Thoughts in Different Shades

To Lee & T.K.
Thank you for your support.
May God continue to bless you both.
Love,
—Victory

Victory Gentry

Thoughts in Different Shades

Copyright © 2024 by Victory Gentry

All rights reserved. No part of this publication may be reproduced, stored in a retrieval system, or transmitted, in any form or by any means, except as may be expressly permitted by the 1976 Copyright Act or by Victory Gentry in writing.

ISBN: 978-1-78324-348-8
ISBN: 978-1-78324-356-3 (ebook)

This book is a work of fiction. Any resemblance to actual persons, living or dead, events or locales is entirely coincidental.

Book design by Wordzworth
www.wordzworth.com

DEDICATION

These writings are an accumulation of my thoughts from my many years of being who I am and my many random thoughts. Some are joyful and some are melancholy but all are thoughtful. With this in mind I would like to dedicate this book to my wife Johnnie, my four children Alisha, Tyler (Emily), Jonathan, and Justin, and my five grandchildren Sean, Brandon Elliot, Tyler Jr., and Rumer. A special thanks to Johann Burke of Louisville KY, who has relentlessly read and reread my written thoughts and given constructive criticism when needed.

INTRODUCTION

I began writing this collection of poems around 1981 and at my early stage of writing. I was struggling with completing most of my poems. I would start one and lose thoughts of what I was trying to say within the poem. It was happening over and over again until I asked this one particular guy. I did not know this guy personally, but I saw him several times on the campus of Tennessee State University. During the late seventies and early eighties he was known to do yoga and to write poetry.

    I happened to see him one day walking on Jefferson Street (the part adjacent to the campus of TSU) and stopped him. I proceeded to share with him my dilemma of not being able to complete my poems and would often lose thought of what I was trying to say within them. This guy looked me in the eyes and asked me one question "who was I writing for?" Not knowing how to answer the question, I stood there in silence and before I could say anything, he spoke (as if he did not want me to say the wrong thing). While speaking, he took his long index finger and started pointing at my chest as if he was touching my heart and said to me, write for yourself young brother. If you are writing for yourself and you like it, then it's good. I took that advice and stopped writing, trying to prove to the world that I am a great writer with heavy thoughts, and trying to appease others. It was then when I began to complete my thoughts and was able to explain within my poems what they were saying.

    Thank You Yoga Man!!!!

CONTENTS

"Am I"	8	Driving at Dawn	30
Just Because	10	Nothing Left	38
We Are Friends	12	We Give Them Reason	40
Black Is Not White	14	Shadow	42
Sounds	16	Devastating Beauty	44
Black Widow	18	She Is My Mother	46
9/11	22	A Parent's Love	48
Ole Massa	24	To: William	50
Close Friends	26	Thank You	52
Can I	28		

"Am I"

Am I the hero
Am I the coward
Or am I the lucky one who just happen to survive

I went off to war in a far away land
Fighting for something that belongs to no man
I lost some friends; some good men had to die
And there were some good men who just barely survive

Am I the hero
Am I the coward
Or am I the lucky one who just happen to survive

No one saw the tears flow from my eyes
No one felt the feelings I had to hide
Scared of dying in that God forsaken land
No one knows or trying to understand

Am I the hero
Am I the coward
Or am I the lucky one who just happen to survive

—Victory—

Just Because

Just because we are friends
I give you this little token of my love
Just because we are close
I pray for you, to the heavens above
Just because you are who you are
I think of you when I wish upon a star
Just because the smile on your face
My heart cries out with
God's Mercy and Grace
Just because

—Victory—

We Are Friends

We sometimes fuss and fight
Almost never see things in the same light
But as the day slowly comes to the end
We are still friends

You always say that I'm late
I always say that auguring is your best trait
But like the sun gives up to the moon
Our friendship is always in tune

The cheapest man I am to you
And leaving my pockets dry is all you do
But as the moon goes in, and dawn comes around
You are still a good friend that I have found

-Victory-

Black Is Not White

Diluted sounds from within
Woke me once again
Once strong but now thin
Is it I who committed a sin

With an finite scream
Of a silent dawn
I was shaken from a dream
As if I was spinning a long yarn

Dusk went and night came
Visions darken went to shame
Tears falling like a rolling river
As my heart is harden like a lion never to be tame

My body is weary
And my mind is tired
I cannot, will not!
Entertain exhaustion for my soul is fired
As I envision a new generation
When only my attributes are umpired

Black is not white and white is not black

—Victory—

Sounds

Clang, clang, clang was the sound of the chains
Wanting my mind, my soul, and my body
Nothing I could do, but to cry lawdy, lawdy, lawdy

Crack, crack, crack was the sound of the whip
Wanting my soul, my body, and my mind
Nothing I could do, but to hold on to my humankind

Tic, tic, tic was the sound of the clock on the wall
Wanting my mind, my body, and my soul
Time wasting and I'm hasting to be old

Shush, shush, shush was the sound of the closing school door
Not wanting my mind, my body, or my soul
Boldly not educating me because of hair of wool

Clang, clang, clang is the sound of the jail cell

—Victory—

Black Widow

The first time I saw you
I didn't know where to start
You shot an arrow into the sky
It pierced me straight in my heart
Cupid's job fell into your hand
Snatching and tearing me apart
Making me your man

The second time I saw you
The arrow fell from my heart
Hoping that it would make me free
While waiting for my healing to start
I was convince that what I felt so surreal
Knowing scars don't heal that come from a banshee
While splitting and ripping my soul apart

The third time I saw you,
I wanted to depart
The wounds were deep, as deep as the sea
I was blind, and visionless from the start
I am not strong, and even less wise
Weeping tears from my heart
Cementing me in being your prize

The fourth time I saw you
Again I didn't know where to start
And you laugh, and you laugh, and you laugh
Knowing by now I have all, but fell apart
And you laugh, and you laugh, and you laugh
With your cold, cold black heart
It was then when the scales fell from my eyes
Only to show me your black widow disguise

-Victory-

9/11

On September 11, 2001
They took a bite out of the Apple
But they fail to reach the core

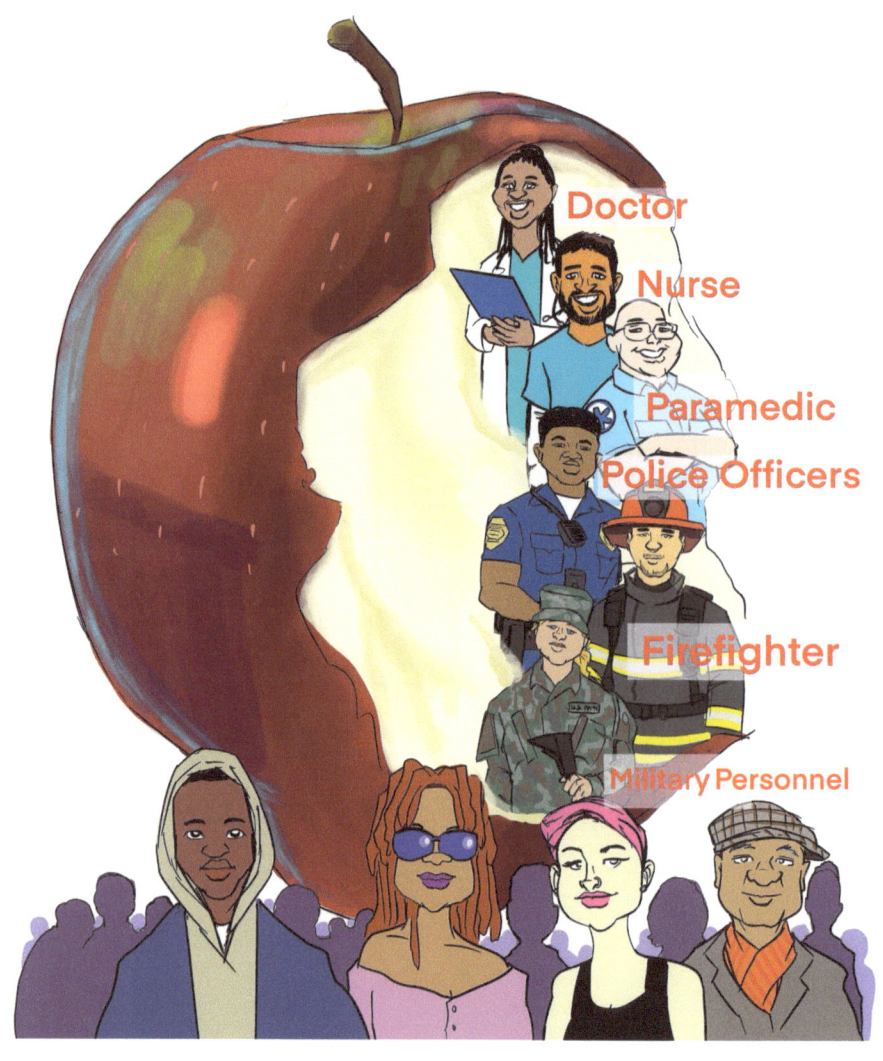

Americans

We are a nation of many people, but when needed we are;

One Nation Indivisible!

Ole Massa

Run Johnny boy run; don't let Ole Massa see you no more
Be as quiet as a mouse
Cause ole massa coming from the house
Swim like a fish and run like a deer
Ole Massa can see you far and near

Run Johnny boy run; don't let Ole Massa beat you no more
Hide from Ole Massa's dog
Lay down by the rotten log
Wade in the muddy waters
So you won't be one of Ole Massa slaughters

Run Johnny boy run; don't let Ole Massa see you no more
Run at night
Rest at light
Run Johnny boy run
Freedom is your right

—Victory—

Close Friends

Close friend that is all I will ever be,
is a close friend that is all you will ever think of me
You told me from the start that your love is for another
Knowing that I would never set you free
I was holding you in my dreams, now and forever
Knowing that we will never be
Close friend that is all I will ever be,
is a close friend that is all you will ever think of me
I let my heart run wild and free hoping
That you will belong to me
I gave you all, all that I had
All the love I had to give
Close friend that is all I will ever be,
is a close friend that is all you will ever think of me
Close friend that is all I will ever be too you
Is a close friend that is all I will ever be

-Victory-

Can I

Can I sing you a love song
Can I tell you a fairy tale
Can I sing you a happy song of love

Can I tell you a story
About a man in his glory
When he found his lucky charm
When he held her tight in his arm

Can I sing you a love song
Can I tell you a fairy tale
Can I sing you a happy song of love

Can I tell you a story
About a woman in her glory
When she found her king
When he ask her to be his queen

Can I sing you a love song
Can I tell you a fairy tale
Can I sing you a happy song of love

—Victory—

Driving at Dawn
"Please Help My Momma"

Written By

-Victory-

It was the fourth month of school that year, when I was told that I would be getting two new elementary students to ride the school bus that I was

assigned to drive. They would be waiting at the bus stop on 18th and Johnson in the morning.

This bus stop was located in a neighborhood where only brown skinned children would ride the bus, and they would be standing in the street because the bushes in the yard next to the corner had overgrown onto the sidewalk. I made a report, but was told that there was nothing they could do because the bushes were on private property.

The street sign was hanging perpendicular to the street and it

30

was just hanging on, waiting for someone to hit the pole one more time. It was hard to believe that this was a doorway for a better life for these students who were being bused to a school in the part of town that they were not familiar with. For some of them, I was the last face they would see, that would remind them of themselves for the next six hours.

The next morning, like clockwork at 8:43am, the big yellow lights on the school bus started flashing. The bus stopped, the stop sign swung out, and the doors opened. The students knew as they entered upon this bus; they were expected to speak. "Good morning Mr. Rick", they said as they were getting on the bus. As they were walking to their seats, I could hear them saying, "Mr. Rick always makes us say good morning when we get on the bus and goodbye when we get off going home." "Yea, James the outspoken one on the bus said, "It's too early for all of that. Dang nobody feels like talking this early in the morning. I liked the other bus driver better anyway. She didn't say anything to us and we didn't have to say anything to her."

I saw the two new students standing on the sidewalk near the overgrown bushes; they seemed to be standing all alone and waiting for the other students to get on the bus. I noticed there was not a parent on the stop with them. I could tell that they were standing there with the fear of the unknown, but it also looked as if they had done this before, or something like this. I do understand that a lot of these parents do not stand on the bus stop with their children, but that's not the case when the students are new.

As the new students got on the bus, I stopped them and asked what their names were.

The girl spoke first. I could easily tell that she was the politician of the family. She was talking fast using body language and hand motions. She told me her name was Sam and that it was short for Samantha, and that she was named after her grandmother, and that her brother's name was Robert Jr.

She was tall, but thin for her age. Their clothes were clean, but very wrinkled as if they were not folded, but left in a pile after they were washed and dried. While she was walking through the bus aisle, she spoke to the other students when she walked by them as if she was searching for a friend. I could tell her brother was younger than her by a couple of years and he was her opposite. He did not speak as he got on the bus, but he raised his head for a brief moment and we made eye contact. It wasn't the type of contact that was saying good morning or hi. It was as if he was looking through me. He did not speak to any of the students as he went by them. When his sister found an empty seat she stood by it and gave him an invitation to sit down first and then she sat down beside him. He did not slide close to the window, but just enough so she could sit down. It looked as if he was almost sitting in her lap. Again he did not look up; he immediately started staring out of the window while Sam tried to start some conversations with the other students.

After a few weeks I finally got a chance to meet Sam and Robert Jr.'s parents on two different occasions. First I met their mother at the bus stop. I could tell that Sam was a little embarrassed. Her mother came to the bus stop with a nightgown and a housecoat that was very loose fitting and they seemed too big for her as if she lost a lot of weight. She greeted me very politely and told me that she was Sam and Robert Jr.'s mother and that she had custody over them and not their father, and that he lives out of town with his mother. Why she chose to make a point and tell me that she had custody over Sam and her brother, and that the father lives with his mother. I didn't know, but I could tell that she was educated and that at one time she might have had a lot going for her, but this morning she looked like she was depending on something to help her make it through some days. I made the conversation short because she was making me feel uncomfortable being dressed like that in front of me and students. I felt as if she was allowing the wind to blow her loose fitting clothing open trying to get my attention.

Their father came by a few weeks later. I could tell that Sam was excited and proud that he was at her bus stop with her. She introduced him to me with a big smile on her face and with excitement "Mr. Rick, Mr. Rick! This is my dad, and guess what? His name is Sam too!" He interrupted Sam and told me that he was named after his mother also. He seemed to be doing better than Sam and Robert Jr.'s mother, but not much. He told me that he just got out of the military a few months ago, and that his mother was living with him. I was not sure about that; because Sam's mother told me that he was the one living with someone, but that was not my concern. He was also making excuses for why his children were not living with him. I guess trying to get me to understand his predicaments. Again, I kept this conversation short because I had a schedule to keep. As I was pulling off in the school bus I couldn't help but wonder; how did Robert Jr. become a junior?

A couple of months went by and every day the students would be in a great debate about who has the most of nothing. Sam would be the loudest on some days; she wasn't trying to prove that she had the most of nothing. She was trying to prove that she and her brother weren't less than nothing. Like all of the other students, she would compare what she didn't have to what the others didn't have, and all of the things that their parents were going to give them, the places they were going, and what their older siblings were doing if they had any. Most of it, if not all, was hopes and dreams.

A few weeks later again, like clockwork, at 8:43am, the big yellow lights on the school bus started flashing, but something was different about this particular morning. It was spring and it was wet, cold, and gray. I could barely see a few of the students on the bus stop through the morning fog as the bus was pulling up towards them. I stopped the school bus, the stop sign on the side of the bus swung out, and the doors opened.

The few students that were on the bus stop began to enter the bus and as usual they spoke, but they spoke with hesitation, and I was slow to speak back because I was somewhat confused by their actions as they were getting on the bus. I asked where everyone was. One of them spoke as they were pointing, and said something is going on down there by Sam's home.

If I was at another bus stop. It may have been odd to me because so many students were not at the bus stop, but not this bus stop. By this time of the year it has become a habit for me not to pull off the bus stop if all of the students were not there. I had become too familiar with the students and how their family function in the morning.

James the outspoken one, with all of the mouth and comebacks that any old man on the street would love to have, would come out of his home four out of the five days of school late, eating on something and screaming at the same time "here I come, don't pull off Mr. Rick!" He wasn't the only one. It seemed like they all would take turns being late to the bus stop. I knew my bus compound did not approve of waiting, but I also knew my students, and how important it was for these students to be in school. Therefore, if waiting a few minutes assured that these students would be in school rather than being at home doing nothing, then I was going to wait a few minutes.

At once, I heard a loud piercing scream. It seemed as if it was right beside me, but in fact it was in the middle of the street that was adjacent to the bus stop by Sam's home. I inched the bus forward a little to allow me to see down that street. It was still foggy and hard to see. I could only see shadows and outline shapes of people. Some were tall and some were short. I heard a lot of voices screaming. Some were young voices, and some were older voices. Some of the voices sounded like they were crying and some of them were shouting profanity and threatening language. All of a sudden, I heard another voice. It came from the porch of a house away from the crowd in the street. It was a loud voice, much louder than the voices in the street shouting "I'm calling the police on all of y'all niggers. It's too early in the morning for all of  this shit." Then I notice a small crowd coming towards the school bus. It was the rest of my students that were supposed to be at the bus stop, running towards the bus hollowing "don't leave us Mr. Rick!"

As they were getting on the bus, some of them were out of breath, some were laughing, but all of them were trying to out-talk each other about what was going on down the street and they were getting louder and louder. They were so excited that none of them said good morning as they got on the bus, but they were trying to explain to me and each other what happened on the street.

As I reached to pull the bus doors shut, I noticed two more students walking very slow in the fog. They were holding each other with the taller one arm around the shorter one's shoulder. They were walking as if they did not have anywhere to go and didn't care if I pulled off or not. I motioned for them to speed up because I was running behind schedule, but as they got closer I saw that they were going as fast as they could because they were crying, and holding on to each other as if that is all that they had.

Before they made it to the bus, James,the outspoken one who was one of the students that were already on the bus, ran up front saying "Mr. Rick, Mr. Rick, man my momma and daddy was" I stopped him mid-sentence, before he could finish I told him to go back and sit down. By then, the two students were at the door and I recognized it was Sam and her brother Robert Jr.

   They stood there for a moment and Sam Looked up at me with tears in her eyes, and her arm still around her brother's shoulders. She was in full protection mode, not knowing that she needed protection herself. At that moment Sam began to scream. Not screaming at me, but screaming out of fear. "My momma needs some help. All of them are fighting my momma." At the same time I overheard James talking to one of the students in the back; as if he was bragging. "Yea, my momma, daddy, and my big sister were fighting Sam's momma. They were going to beat her ass." I immediately told James to sit down, watch his mouth and be quiet.

   "Mr. Rick, Mr. Rick!" Sam continued shouting, "can you help my momma? They are going to hurt her." Sam's shouting soon turned into crying alongside her brother and I heard and felt each tear as they fell as heavy boulders falling on my heart. I told her the only thing I could do right now is to call my bus compound and have them call the police. I convince Sam and Robert Jr. to get on the bus for their safety. I got on the bus radio and called the bus compound to make a report and to ask for police support, but within minutes the fight was over. I told Sam that the fight was over and that I saw her mother go into their house and that we needed to head to school.

   Sam and her brother were still terrified and crying as they got on to the bus. Her eyes were full of tears and her lips were shaking, she did not speak as she got on the bus. She went towards the back of the bus along with her brother walking behind her. She stopped at an empty seat in the middle of the bus and unlike she usually does, she did not allow her brother to sit down first. Sam sat in the seat before she let her brother sit down. She positioned herself so that she could look straight into the bus rear view mirror so I could see her reflection in the mirror. Her face and eyes were saying *"please help my momma. Don't let them hurt her."*

It was a long ride to the school after that bus stop. Most of the students seemed to be unconcerned with what had happened at the bus stop, but James and a few of the students seemed to be excited and charged up with what happened. The more I tried to get them to calm down and stop talking about what happened, the louder they got. As if they wanted Sam and her brother to hear what they were saying.

Sam and her brother Robert Jr. continued to cry the entire way to school. Upon arriving at the school, I called my bus compound again and asked them to call the school to see if Sam and Robert Jr. teachers could meet them on the bus this morning. I let all of the students off except for Sam and Robert Jr. until I saw their teachers coming towards the bus. I motioned for them to get off the bus, and again they started moving very slow. The way they were sitting in the seat Robert Jr. got out first and Sam was following behind him, but very slow. Robert Jr. reached the first step and started going down the steps. Just as Sam was getting ready to go down the steps, she turned around, looked at me, and grabbed me around my neck crying and said that she didn't want to go to school. She kept repeating "I want to go home. I want to go home." The teachers started running towards the bus and asked what was wrong? I explained to the teachers and the principal what was going on. I looked at them and their eyes were full of tears. One of the teachers wiped her eyes, but for the most part they were able to hold their tears back. They put their arms around both Sam, and Robert Jr. and escorted them off the bus and into the school.

After explaining to the principal and teachers what had happened at the bus stop, it was time for me to head back to the bus compound. I never saw Sam and her brother Robert Jr. again. All I can remember is the last look she gave me when she reached the school door and turned around and looked at me. All I could see from her face were her lips moving saying, *"Please help my momma."*

Nothing Left

Inner feelings, the peaceful and the wild
One is scared of finding himself never again a child
With a small frame and a body of a juvenile
This one must conquer the world without a smile
As mother dies in his arms
Strength flows from his eyes, leaving no trace of charm
Mother dead and Father gone
This child was left to bear his own
The job he must do, and see it done
This child is only nine, yet he has a son
One took him and one took his brother
The only thing they had left was each other
With nowhere to run and nowhere to hide
This cold, cold world has left nothing inside

–Victory–

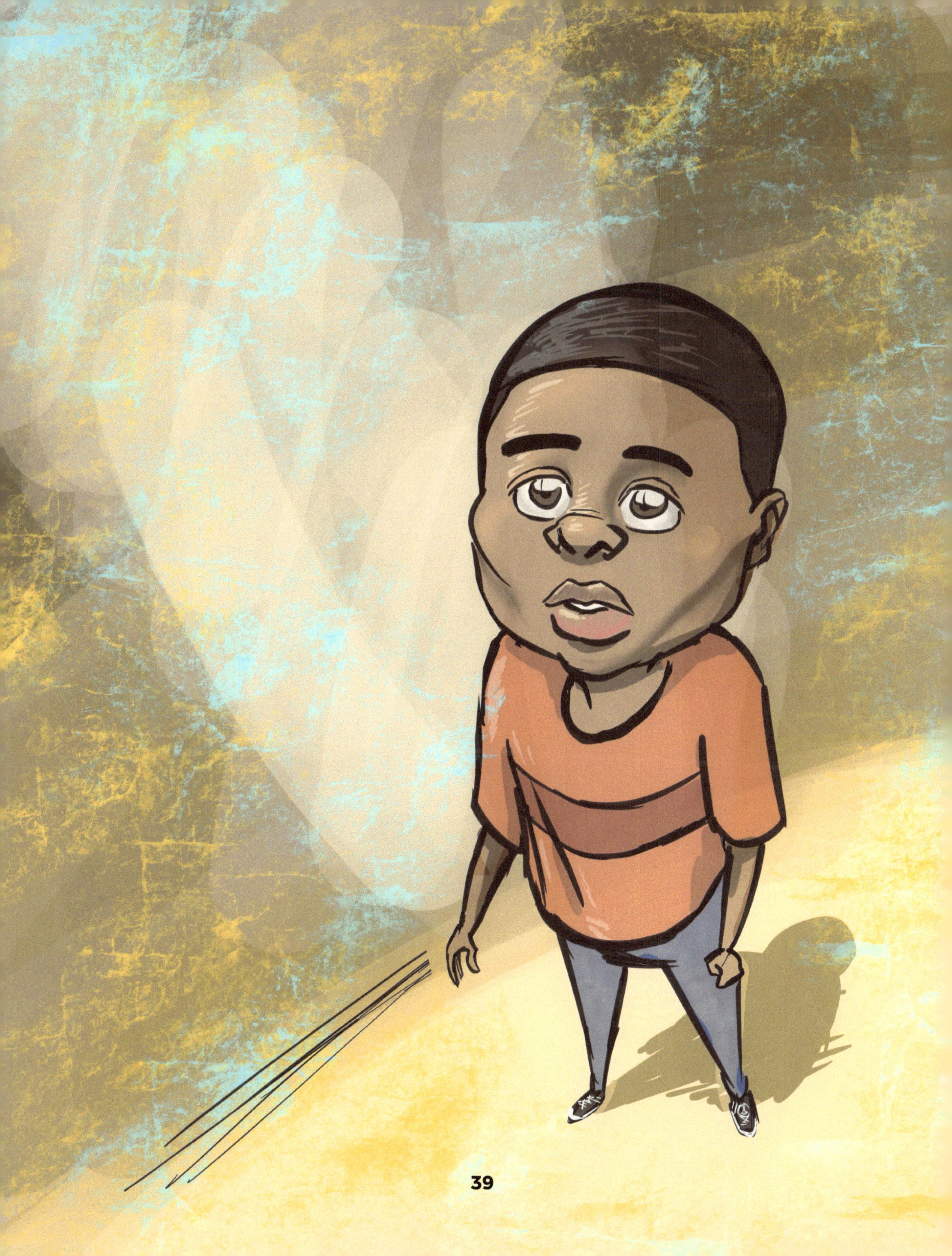

We Give Them Reason
(To Us)

Rape, Steal, Kill
Is that all we do?
No!
Then let's look at us

Run, Quit, Abandon
Is that all we do?
No!
Then let's look at us

Laugh, Sleep, Play
Is that all we do?
No!
Then let's look at us

Showing our draws, Wearing our gold, Putting Michael on our feet
Is that all we do?
No!
Then let's look at us

We give them reasons!!

–Victory–

41

Shadow
To: my Grandson B

In my shadow I chose to hide
In my shadow I can rest inside
In my shadow I can be what I want to be
In my shadow I am just me

In my shadow you can't see me
In my shadow I'm not part of your tree
In my shadow I don't have to follow your degree
In my shadow you have to just let me be

In my shadow there's no controversy
In my shadow I'm who I want to be
In my shadow I'm not hard to see
In my shadow I am free

In my shadow I don't have to run or flee
In my shadow I hold the key
In my shadow I don't have to plea
I my shadow I know to whom I bend my knee

In my Shadow!

—Victory—

Devastating Beauty

Your hair is like the long lazy river
and as smooth as the breeze flowing through the valley.
Your eyes are like the black coal hidden deep in the African mountains.
Your skin is as smooth as a butterfly dancing from flower to flower.
Your lips are as soft as the petals, on a Mother's day pink rose.
Your legs are as long as the great rivers flowing from river to river.
Your shape is the art of no man's blueprint and no man's imagination .
Your beauty is devastating
But oh! I dare not take your beauty for weakness, for you are stalwart
and your tongue can carry the venom of a deadly serpent.
Your thoughts can be as cold as the frozen waters in the Tundra and
your reflexes can be as quick as a stalking cat after her prey.
Oh I dare not! Take your beauty for a weakness.
Your beauty is devastating

−Victory−

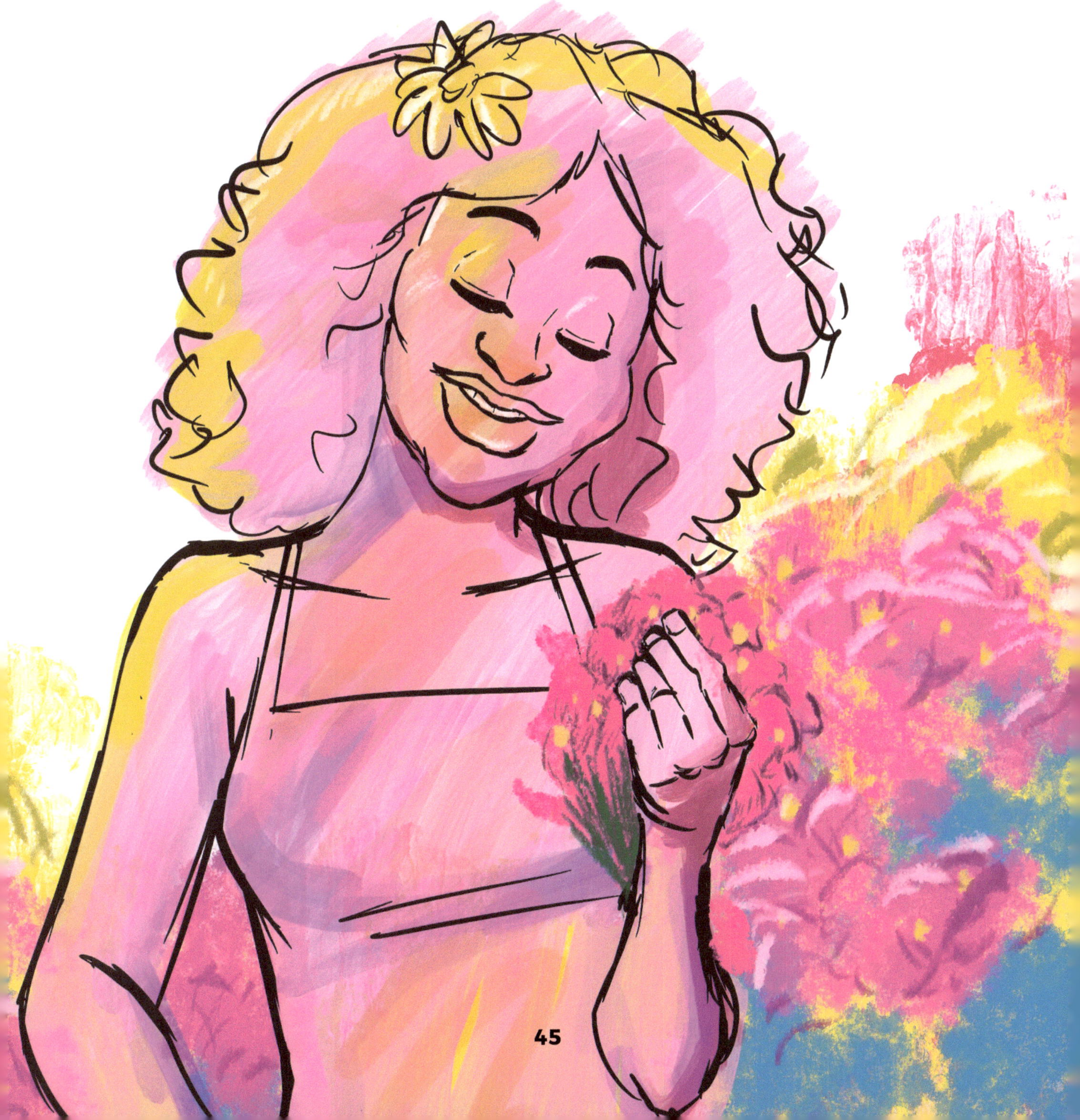

She Is My Mother

She is my mother
The one who taught me before I can walk I must learn to crawl
The one who is always there to pick me up when I fall
She is my mother
The one who sees me in need, and gives me a helping hand
When there is no one else, she is there willing to understand
She is my mother
The one who taught me right from wrong
The one who gave me strength to stand tall and be strong
She is my mother
The one who gave me plenty of love
The one who taught me to keep my faith in the one above
She is my mother!

—Victory—

47

A Parent's Love

Love is a mother's love
Like a tree in the spring
In preparation of life for her offspring

Love is a father's love
Like a tree in the summer
Standing tall and firm protecting all that is around

Love is a mother's love
Like a tree in autumn
Giving up everything she has for the ones she loves

Love is a father's love
Like a tree in the winter
Unclothe and enduring the harsh elements for the ones he loves

Love is a parent's love

—Victory—

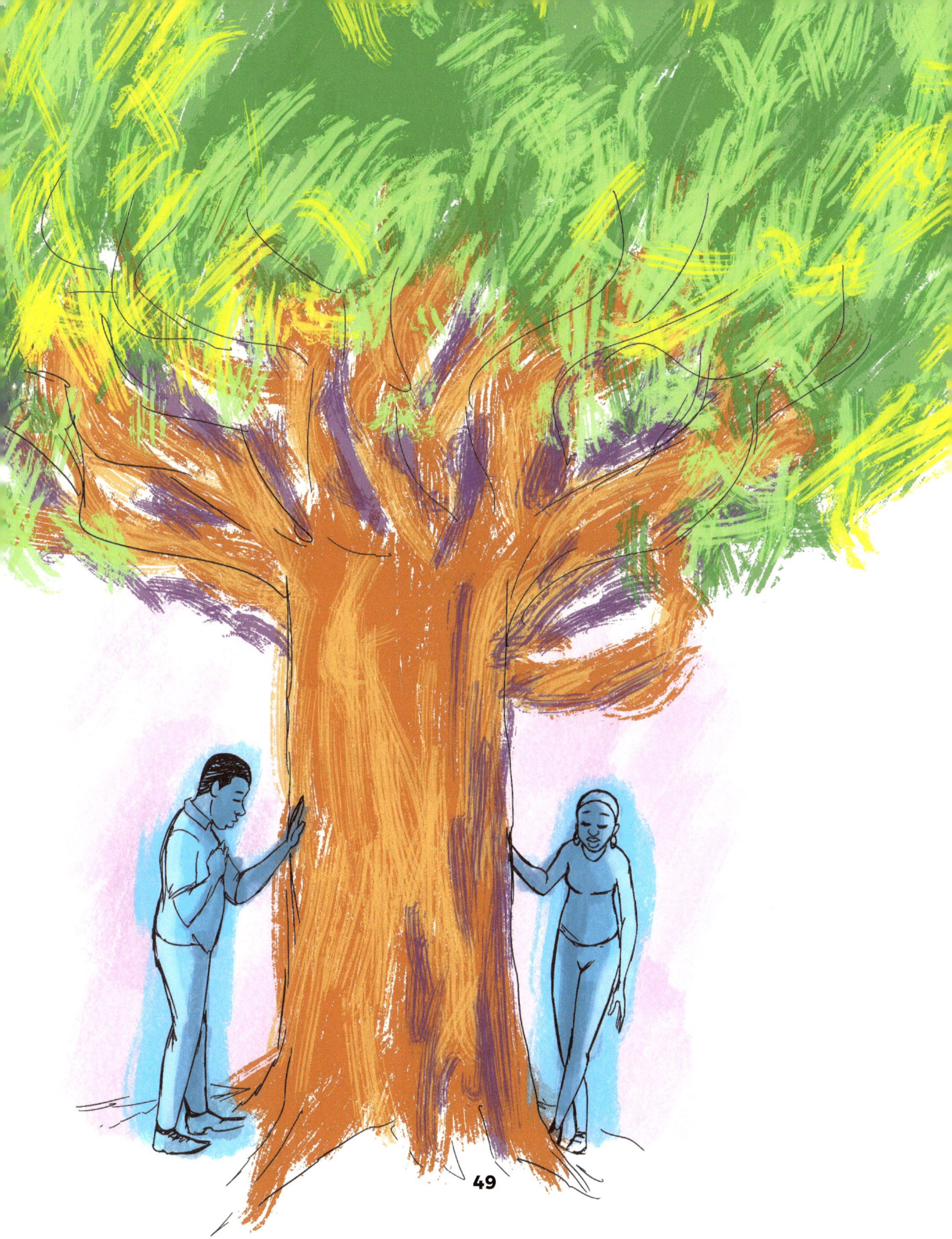

To: William

There are a million thoughts of you, and a million tears will fall
No matter how hard we try, we know we must let you go

For God's love is great, and does not plateau
Now there is no more pain for you to know

You have spread your wings and taken flight
Our God in heaven knew it was time for you to unite

—Victory—

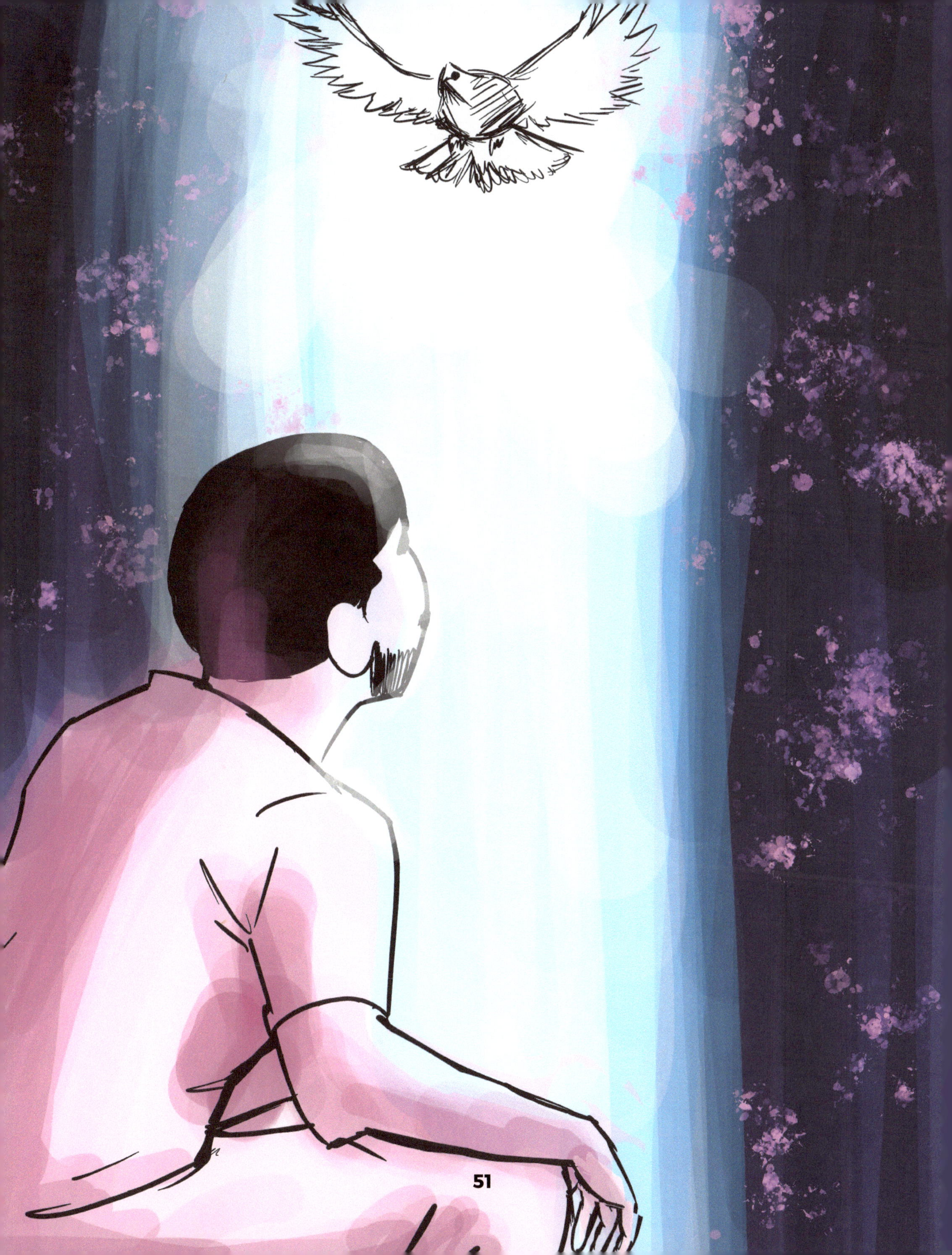

Thank You

Thank you for one more day
Thank you for saving my soul
You didn't have to let me rise
You didn't have to open my eyes
Thank you

—Victory—

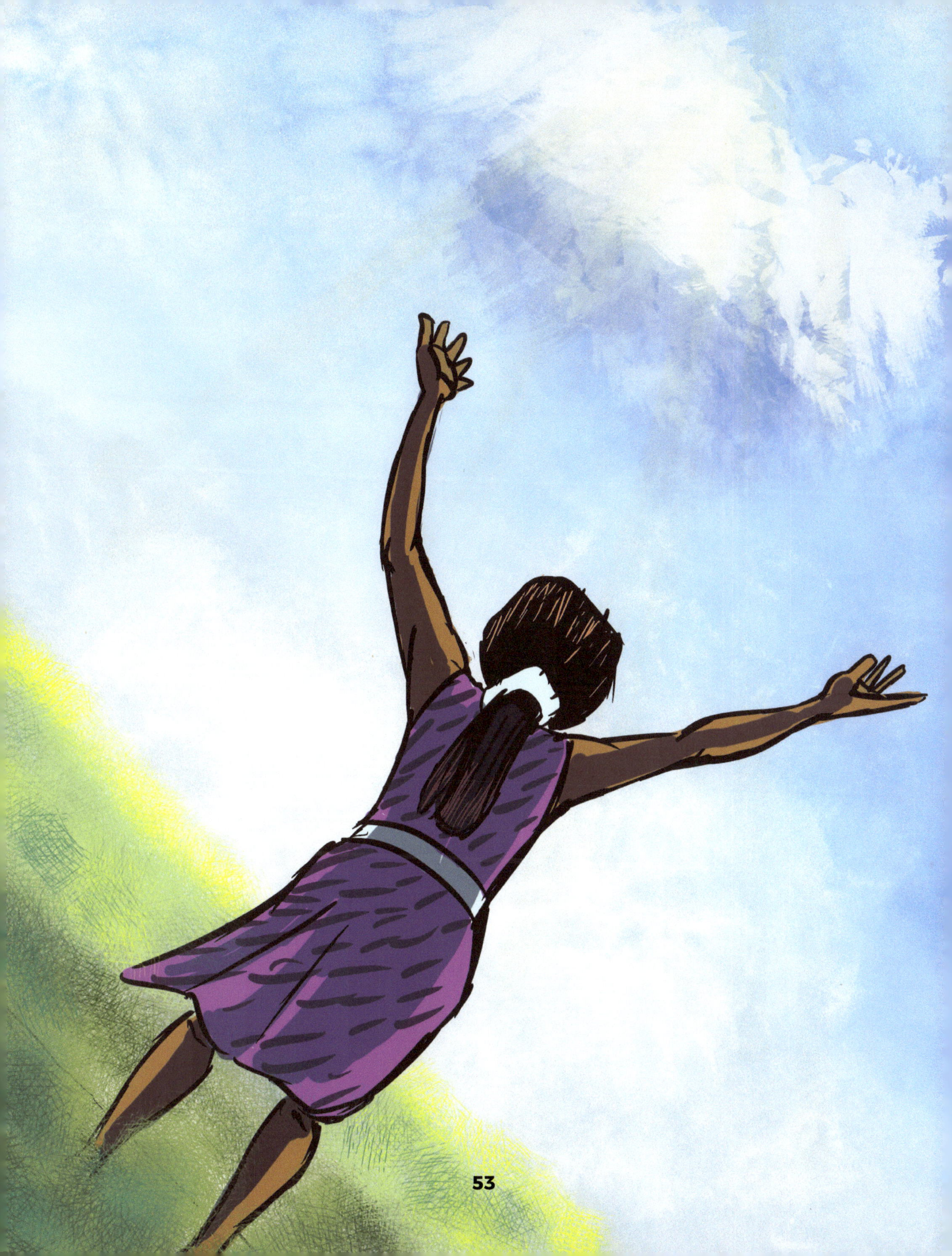

ABOUT THE ILLUSTRATOR

Randy Gray is a caricature artist and illustrator from Louisville, KY. He has a degree in graphic design from the University of Kentucky. When he isn't spending time with his wife and kids he is most likely drawing or exercising.

ABOUT THE AUTHOR

Victory R. Gentry is a writer and author of fiction and poetry books for children and adults. Born in Nashville, TN but resides in Louisville Ky. He is the last of five siblings and enjoyed listening to the stories from older siblings. He is married with four children and five grandchildren that he enjoys telling and sharing stories with.